Little Eenie has asked his friend Meenie to get a piece of cheese for him. Can you help Meenie reach the piece of cheese?

The caterpillar is looking for an apple to fill its belly.
Do you see an apple? Can you help the caterpillar find it?

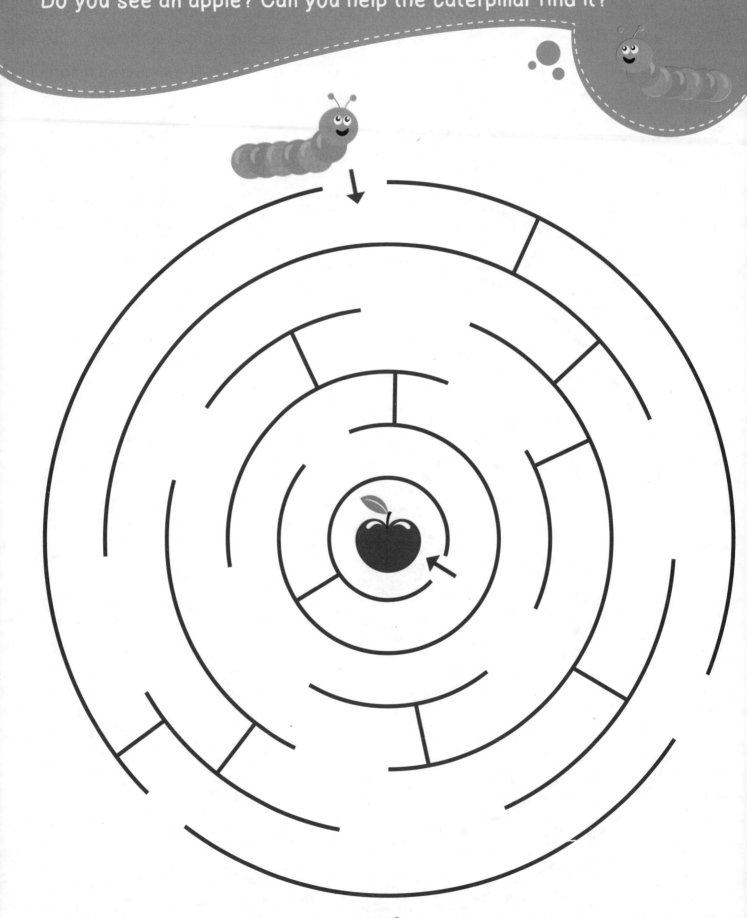

The puzzle pieces are worried for their missing friend.
Help them reach their friend by finding the right path.

Little Prince is looking for his beautiful Princess.
Can you help him reach her by finding the right path?

4

It's Christmas time! Santa Claus is here to wish the snowman a merry Christmas. Can you help Santa find the snowman?

Mama Cow is looking for grass to feed her calf.
Can you help her find it?

Baby Bear wants to have some honey. He needs your help to reach his jar of honey. Can you find the right way?

HONEY

HONEY

Freshly cooked chicken is waiting for Mr and Mrs Hollycook. Help them find their way back home before the chicken gets cold.

Dr Harry and Dr Larry are running late for the hospital. Can you help them reach on time by finding the right way?

These mischievous monkeys are going to a beach, but have lost their way. Can you help them?

It's Christmas Eve! Baby Penguin is racing on skates with his friends. Help him finish the race.

The potion is boiling, and the witch has the final ingredient! Can you help her reach the cauldron in time?

Help the rabbit find its way through the maze
to reach the carrot.

Pirate Johnny and his friends are looking for treasure.
Can you help them find it?

A group of penguins have decided to sing Christmas carols with Santa Claus. Can you help each of them find their way to Santa?

Answers (Pages 1–15)

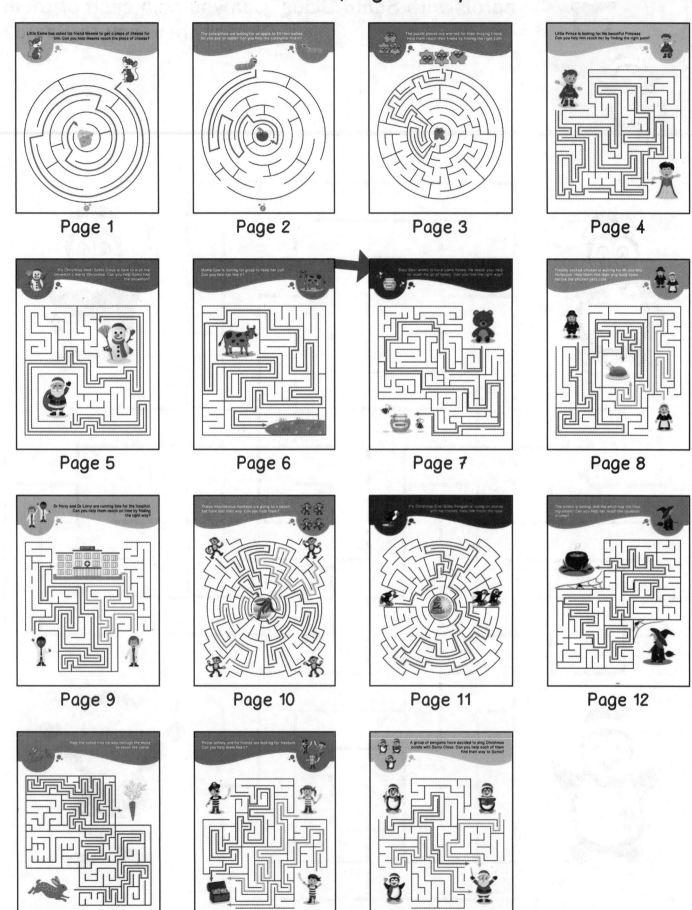

Page 1

Page 2

Page 3

Page 4

Page 5

Page 6

Page 7

Page 8

Page 9

Page 10

Page 11

Page 12

Page 13

Page 14

Page 15